Listen to the Birds
An Introduction to Classical Music
Music selection and explanatory notes **Ana Gerhard** Illustrations **Cecilia Varela**

Listen to the Birds

With their many remarkable qualities, birds capture people's imagination, perhaps more so than any other animal. Throughout history, they have represented a myriad of concepts, such as freedom (wings), peace (the dove), power (the eagle and the condor), spring (the swallow), purity (the swan), innocence (chicks), evil (the crow), death (the vulture), and wisdom (the owl).

There are close to 10,000 known species of birds of all shapes, colours and sizes, but their most notable feature is their feathers. Certain feathers were so beautiful and revered that North American Native tribe chiefs used them to make splendid multi-coloured panaches that they wore as a crown, symbolizing power and wealth.

Most birds can fly, an ability that has inspired many attempts by humans to invent mechanisms to do the same.

Song is another distinctive quality of these winged creatures that we so admire. Birds do not have vocal cords; rather, they have an organ called the "syrinx," which allows them to produce a wide range of sounds. This organ is made up of various vibrating membranes, a reverberation capsule and several muscles that control its movement. The syrinx is located where the trachea splits in two, which allows many songbirds to produce two or more sounds simultaneously.

Barring a few exceptions, birdsong is reserved for males. They mainly sing to attract females or to mark their territory. Each species has its own distinct song, but some have the ability to expand their repertoire by imitating the songs of other birds. Research has shown, that in some species, the repertoire is innate, while in others, it is acquired by the young as they imitate their parents. Certain bird couples sing together, coordinating their song beautifully.

Some scientists and historians believe that humans' desire to imitate birdsong may be at the root of music. Even if it is just a theory, it is indisputable that several composers drew their inspiration from birds, either by subtly evoking their voice or movements, mimicking their melodies with various instruments, or incorporating birdsongs recorded in nature into their works.

1 The Goldfinch

Il Gardellino (Antonio Vivaldi)
Concerto for flute and orchestra

The goldfinch—*gardellino* in Italian—is a very common bird with an exceptionally colourful plumage. Its face is almost entirely covered with a red mask, which contrasts with its black eyes and whitish beak. Its beige body accentuates its black and yellow wings as well as its black tail, with its white-spotted tip.

It is rare to spot a goldfinch flying at a high altitude. It is very sociable, and generally travels in a flock. Its melodious song, consisting of fast, high-pitched trills followed by longer low-pitched sounds, is so enjoyed that it is not uncommon to find this species in captivity.

In his concerto *Il Gardellino,* Vivaldi uses the flute to conjure the song of the goldfinch.

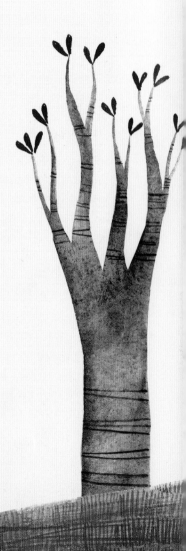

2 Spring

La Primavera (Antonio Vivaldi)
Concerto for violin and orchestra

In 1726, Antonio Vivaldi published *Il cimento dell'armonía e dell'invenzione,* an expansive work consisting of 12 concertos for violin and orchestra. The first four concertos of this set are the famous *Four Seasons: Spring, Summer, Autumn* and *Winter,* which illustrate different aspects of the seasons through elements of musical language.

Each of these four concertos is accompanied by a sonnet that expresses in words what the music is meant to evoke. Vivaldi actually included the verses corresponding to the musical passage on the score to avoid any ambiguity.

The sonnet that accompanies Spring is as follows:

> *Springtime is upon us. The birds celebrate her return with festive song, and murmuring streams are softly caressed by the breezes.*
>
> *Thunderstorms, those heralds of Spring, roar, casting their dark mantle over heaven. Then they die away to silence, and the birds take up their charming songs once more.*
>
> *On the flower-strewn meadow, with leafy branches rustling overhead, the goat-herd sleeps, his faithful dog beside him.*
>
> *Led by the festive sound of rustic bagpipes, nymphs and shepherds lightly dance beneath the brilliant canopy of spring.*

The first two verses of the sonnet are the backbone of the concerto's first movement. At each of the two bird references, the solo violin, first by itself and then accompanied by the rest of the orchestra, mimics bird calls and their melodic songs with its cheerful trills.

3 Birdsong

Le chant des oiseaux (Clément Janequin)
Polyphonic song **for 4 voices**

The lark, the thrush, the starling, the nightingale and the cuckoo,
all very well known for their song, are the protagonists of this piece.
Their melodious warbling announces the arrival of spring, the mating
period during which males compete for females through their calls.

Le chant des oiseaux opens with verses that invite us to delight in
nature's awakening after the cold, gloomy days of winter. Little by little,
the language becomes incoherent and transforms itself to mimic bird
voices and entertain us with cheerful hullabaloo.

Frian, frian, frian, frian, frian, frian...
Tar tar tar tar tar tar tu,
Velecy, velecy,
Ticun, ticun, ticun,
Tu, tu... coqui, coqui, coqui, coqui...,
Fiti, fi ti, quilara, quilara, quilara,
Teo coqui coqui, si ti si ti,
Turry, turry, turry, qui lara,
Tweet, tweet, tweet...
Oy ty, oy ti, oy ti, teo teo teo teo
Teo teo, etc...

4 Melancholy

Cantus Arcticus (Einojuhani Rautavaara)
Concerto for birds and orchestra

The soloists in this work are the birds of the North Pole: cranes (which look like herons, with their long necks and long feet), skylarks and swans. Unlike the previous pieces, which conveyed the joy of spring, in this second movement, entitled *Melancholy,* you will hear these Nordic birds evoke the sadness and solitude of the wintry landscape.

Cantus Arcticus was composed in 1972 at the request of the University of Oulu. Einojuhani Rautavaara explains that he had already had the idea of composing a concerto for birds and orchestra when he had gone walking in the Lapland bogs, where he had spent many a summer as a child. This is where he recorded the birds whose songs "create a mysterious counterpoint to the rustling of the trees." When he returned home from his excursion, the composer incorporated the recordings of the birds' voices into the instrumental music.

5 The Bird

Peter and the Wolf (Serguëï Prokofiev)
Flute solo

The bird in *Peter and the Wolf* does not belong to a particular species. The first words that come to mind when one thinks of a bird are "light," "delicate" and "nimble"; this is why Prokofiev chose the bird to represent the sound of the flute.

Serguëï Prokofiev composed *Peter and the Wolf* to familiarize children with the sounds of an orchestra. In this work, all the characters in the story are represented by the characteristic timbre of an instrument. The tale's narrative is straightforward: one morning, Peter decides to go for a walk in the meadow, unaware of all the dangers and adventures that await him. Together with his friends (a bird, a duck and a cat), he will have to confront a terrible wolf.

6 Hens and Roosters

The Carnival of the Animals (Camille Saint-Saëns)
A great zoological fantasy

The hen is perhaps the least poetic bird there is, but since the beginning of time, it has been a staple of the human diet. It is also one of the most common birds on the planet (it is estimated that there are more than 13 billion of them!). Hens are sociable birds that have lost the ability to fly.

The hen's cry is not a particularly pleasant sound either. While the rooster lets out his famous "cockadoodle doo" at dawn, to attract females or inform males of the presence of a competitor, the hen cackles every time she lays an egg. That's why the verb "to cackle" also means "to chatter" or "to gossip."

In the second piece of this *fantasy,* which follows the *Royal March of the Lion* for an even greater effect, Camille Saint-Saëns mimics the distinctive sound hens make.

The Carnival of the Animals, which includes 14 pieces representing various animals, was composed by Saint-Saëns in February 1886 as a joke. The work was meant to be performed at his house, by friends, for the carnival. It is said that the composer, fearing that the work was too frivolous and that it would tarnish his reputation as a serious composer, forbade its publication during his lifetime, with the exception of the piece entitled *The Swan*. Upon his death, in accordance with the will of Saint-Saëns, *The Carnival of the Animals* was published in its entirety. It is now one of the composer's most famous works.

7 Aviary

The Carnival of the Animals (Camille Saint-Saëns)
Flute piece

The tenth piece in *The Carnival of the Animals* is not about a particular bird, but about an aviary, that is, a large cage where birds are kept. They are generally found in gardens, parks and zoos; they allow us to see and hear a wide variety of birds of different sizes, colours and shapes that live together and sing in an enclosed area.

The Swan

8

The Carnival of the Animals (Camille Saint-Saëns)
Flute piece

The swan is a large bird belonging to the duck family. Mainly aquatic, it is still part of the only group of birds that can, to a certain extent, use the three means of locomotion: walking, flying and swimming.

Its elegant white plumage, its long delicate neck and its majestic movement in the water have made this animal a symbol of beauty and harmony. This reputation has earned the swan a place in many tales and legends and has inspired fabulous musical works, including *The Swan* from *The Carnival of the Animals*.

In this piece, Saint-Saëns leaves irony and humour aside to write a magnificent elegy led by the cello, accompanied by pianos. It is the only piece from the Carnival that the composer deemed worthy of being published before his death. In 1905, the great Russian ballerina Ana Pavlova performed *The Dying Swan,* a romantic ballet set to the music of Camille Saint-Saëns's *The Swan,* which was met with great success.

9 Dance of the Little Swans

Swan Lake (Pyotr Ilyich Tchaikovsky)
Ballet suite

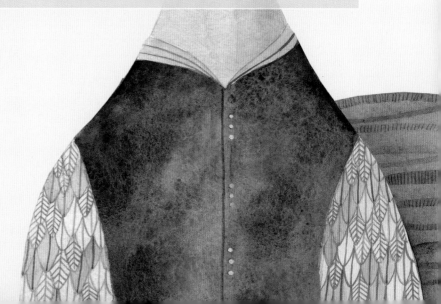

Swans are known around the world for their incomparable beauty, but when we think of their young, the image of the "ugly duckling" is first to come to mind. In the Hans Christian Andersen tale, the ugly duckling is mocked because he is lanky, awkward and rather unattractive, until he notices, seeing his reflection in the water, that he has become a majestic swan. At birth, the young are covered in a light brown down; their beaks are black, their necks are not as elegant or long as those of adults, and most of all, because of their short feet, they have a funny and clumsy walk. In short, they have neither the beauty nor the grace of their parents.

In the second act of *Swan Lake,* four ballerinas appear on the stage. They form a line and, mimicking the sweet walk of the baby swans, who move in close groups as though to protect themselves, move in unison, arms crossed and hands linked.

Today, *Swan Lake* is a an immensely popular ballet, despite the fact that its opening at the Bolshoi Theatre in Moscow in 1877 was a complete flop. Accompanied by a fabulous musical score, it tells the story of Odette, a princess turned into a swan by an evil sorcerer, a spell that can only be broken if a prince pledges his eternal love to her. When Prince Siegfried goes to the lake and falls in love with Odette, who turns back into a human every evening at dusk, she believes her happy ending is imminent. It is at this point in the story that the *Dance of the Little Swans* takes place.

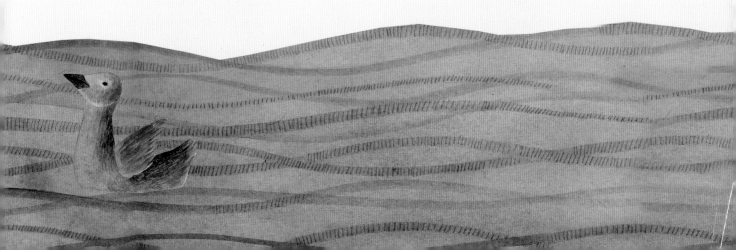

10 Song of the Lark

Album for the Young (Pyotr Ilyich Tchaikovsky)
For piano

The lark is a common bird whose brown spotted plumage provides an excellent camouflage in desert areas, meadows and marshes.

Despite its rather drab appearance, the lark has a remarkable song: its trills and tremolos vary in tone, duration, rhythm and timbre. A single melodic sequence can last up to an hour. As a result of its quality, variety and duration, the lark's song has inspired many an artist.

In his *Album for the Young,* Tchaikovsky included various themes of interest to young children, such as toys, folk songs and imaginary characters. Animals could not be left out, and the lark, whose melodious song can easily be reproduced on the piano, was a natural inclusion.

The *Album for the Young,* which, according to the composer, is a series of short pieces that are easy to listen to and have titles that appeal to children, is inspired by the work of the same name by Robert Schumann, one of the composers that Tchaikovsky admired the most, along with Mozart, Beethoven and Weber.

11 Lark Ascending

Lark Ascending (Ralph Vaughan Williams)
Romance for violin and orchestra

In addition to its musicality, another distinctive characteristic of the lark is that it sings in flight. The male sings more; this is why he expends so much energy when flying. During the mating season, he sings from very high up, increasing the volume as he rises into the air.

To compose this work, Vaughan Williams drew his inspiration from the poem of the same name by George Meredith. The first verse is as follows:

He rises and begins to round,
He drops the silver chain of sound,
Of many links without a break,
In chirrup, whistle, slur and shake.

12 Ballet of the Unhatched Chicks

Pictures at an Exhibition (Modest Mussorgsky)
Piano suite

The term "chicks" is used to describe baby birds, in particular baby hens. After 21 days of incubation, chicks hatch from their shell, but must remain with their mother or in incubation for at least one day to dry off and adapt to their environment. With their small size and yellow down, they embody innocence and vulnerability.

Composed in 1874, the work *Pictures at an Exhibition* is a 15-piece piano suite. However, the orchestral version created by Maurice Ravel is undoubtedly better known.

Mussorgsky drew his inspiration for this work, originally entitled *Hartmann Suite,* from the posthumous exhibition of 10 paintings and writings by artist and architect Viktor Alexandrovich Hartmann, his close friend, who passed away in 1873 at the age of 39. The composer wanted to pay tribute to him by putting into music some of the paintings on exhibit. The suite begins with the piece entitled *Promenade,* which represents the visitor walking through the exhibition. This theme is repeated throughout the work, from one painting to another, and its character changes based on the impression left on the viewer by the painting.

The *Ballet of the Unhatched Chicks* represents the fourth painting; it corresponds to a drawing of a costume for the *Trilby* ballet produced by Hartmann. The music describes the efforts made by chicks to hatch from their eggs; the humour is also reflected in the comical position of the ballerinas, whose movements are hampered by such a costume.

13 Toccata with Cuckoo Scherzo

Toccata con lo scherzo del cucco (Bernardo Pasquini)
For harpsichord

The cuckoo is a bird with decidedly muted colours (brown, grey and white). It is timid and unsociable, living alone in the deep woods.

It is the bird's song that gave it its name. This species has a poor reputation, as the females lay their eggs in other birds' nests in the hope that the latter will adopt the offspring. The cuckoo is nonetheless appreciated by clockmakers. It is said that, originally, the figure that emerged from clocks to strike the hour was a rooster, a bird that is well known for morning awakening. But, reproducing its cockadoodle doo required a complex mechanism, whereas the cuckoo's song, with only two sounds, was much easier to imitate. The first cuckoo clock appeared in 1738.

In this toccata, Pasquini may have been thinking about his students when he decided to use the characteristic song of the cuckoo as a musical joke (scherzo) transcribed in two notes. The first is shorter and more high-pitched, and the second, longer and more accentuated, is one and a half tones lower than the first.

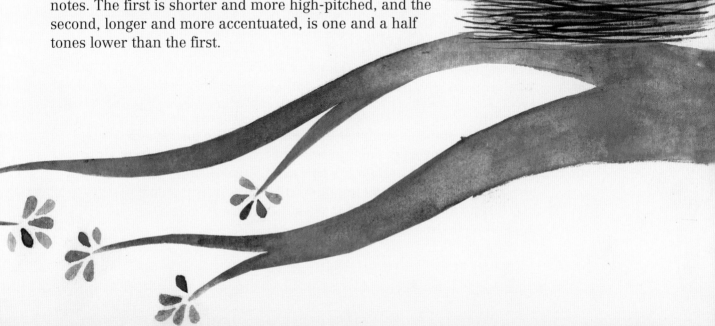

14 The Cuckoo and the Nightingale

The Cuckoo and the Nightingale
(George Frideric Handel)
Concerto for organ and orchestra

As its name suggests, the second movement of this concerto mimics a dialogue between a cuckoo and a nightingale.

The nightingale, a small, grey bird with red spots on its back is highly admired for its song—so much so that, in many languages, calling a human singer "nightingale" is considered a great compliment.
The nightingale symbolizes love in numerous fairy tales and legends, one of the most famous being *The Nightingale and the Rose* by Oscar Wilde. In this tale, the nightingale sacrifices itself to allow a young man to bring his sweetheart a rose.

In the baroque era, the organ was reserved for serious religious music. George Frideric Handel had the idea of taking advantage of the tremendous potential of this instrument by using it as a solo instrument in concertos presented during the interludes of his oratorios. In this new genre, which was well-suited to Handel's character, he played the organ himself, showcasing his talent as an organist and charming the public with his cheerful and lively music. *The Cuckoo and the Nightingale* is the favourite of all these concertos.

15 The Robin

Small Sketches of Birds (Olivier Messiaen)
For piano

The robin is a small, round bird with no neck and covered in grey plumage; however, its chest and face are red. Beneath its friendly appearance, the robin hides the soul of a warrior. The red spot that adorns its breast is actually a territorial warning sign: upon seeing other red breasts, the robin adopts an intimidating stance that intensifies until one of the adversaries leaves, generally before a fight. Its very melodious song is meant to attract females during mating season as well as mark its territory. The robin also sings during fights, incorporating explosive calls, including rapid percussions sung from bushes.

Composed in 1985 as a surprise for his wife, pianist Yvonne Loriod, *Small Sketches of Birds* consists of six short pieces, three of which are entitled *The Robin.* Following his transcriptions, Messiaen attempted to reproduce the true sound of birds in nature using musical elements available to him, an arduous task given that the pleasant chirping that we hear is often made up of microtones emitted at a speed that is impossible for a musician's fingers to reach. To obtain the desired effect, the composer created a combination of tones and rhythms that veer away from the classical language of music.

16 Papageno and Papagena

The Magic Flute (Wolfgang Amadeus Mozart)
Duet for baritone and soprano

Papageno is not an obscure bird species. It is an imaginary character from the opera *The Magic Flute* by Wolfgang Amadeus Mozart. A birdman and bird-catcher, Papageno, whose onomatopoeic name recalls the colourful and likeable parrot—*Papagei* in German—is a comical and good-natured character who dreams of meeting his true love. Towards the end of the piece, in the duet that we will hear, his dream becomes a reality when he is finally united with Papagena, after many hardships.

The storyline of *The Magic Flute* is strongly influenced by fairy tales. Tamino, the main character, is a prince who is sent to rescue the daughter of the Queen of the Night, Princess Pamina, who is being held prisoner in Sarastro's palace. On his mission, Tamino is armed only with a magic flute. He is accompanied by the kind but somewhat cowardly Papageno.

17 Third Movement of Concerto No. 17

Piano Concerto No. 17 (Wolfgang Amadeus Mozart)
For piano and orchestra (theme and variations)

The following piece is oddly associated with the starling, a bird with a small head and a slender body whose black plumage is sprinkled with white spots. Although it mainly feeds on insects and worms by sticking its beak in the grass to locate its prey, the starling is quite comfortable living in the city, where it feeds on leftover food. This great adaptability, however, makes it a nuisance in certain areas. This little bird nevertheless possesses a unique trait: it is capable of mimicking sounds in its environment.

Wolfgang Amadeus Mozart, who had a great love of animals, and particularly birds, from quite a young age, always kept birds as pets. The most well-known of these was a starling that would apparently whistle the main melody of the third movement of his piano concerto No. 17. Some say that Mozart loved this song so much that he transcribed its melody to include it in the concerto that he was writing at the time. Other sources maintain that, on the contrary, this melody was invented by the composer and the starling learned it by hearing it played.

When this starling died, Mozart was so sad that he organized a formal burial in his garden, attended by friends, at which he read a poem that he had composed.

A little fool lies here
Whom I held dear—
A starling in the prime
Of his brief time
Whose doom it was to drain
Death's bitter pain.
Thinking of this, my heart
Is riven apart.
Oh reader! Shed a tear,

You also, here.
He was not naughty, quite,
But gay and bright,
And under all his brag
A foolish wag.
This no one can gainsay
And I will lay
That he is now on high,
And from the sky,

Praises me without pay
In his friendly way.
Yet unaware that death
Has choked his breath,
And thoughtless of the one
Whose rime is thus well done.

18 The Raven

Winter Journey (Franz Schubert)
Lied for voice and piano

The raven is part of the crow family. It has a large flat head, a shiny black coat and very dense plumage. It is omnivorous, raiding the nests of other birds and feeding on insects, scraps and decaying carcasses. Its voice is loud and hoarse with a metallic base tone.

The Raven is the 15th lied of the *Winter Journey* cycle, composed by Schubert on poems by Wilhelm Muller and whose theme is unrequited love. A young man, hurt by unrequited love, embarks on a journey with no destination in the middle of winter to get away from his beloved. The 24 lieder of the work express the thoughts, impressions and feelings of the young man as he wanders alone in the wintry landscape. Coldness, darkness, desolation, and solitude are the predominant themes.

Throughout the first 14 songs, the young man's loneliness is overwhelming. At the 15th lied, we finally feel another presence, but it is not comforting company: it is a raven, a scavenger and bad omen whose black plumage contrasts with the whiteness of the snowy landscape and whose voice is cold and unpleasant, contrary to that of other birds.

The Raven (lyrics)

A raven has flown beside me
Since the day I left the town
Raven, bird of ill-omen
Will you ever leave me?
Do you stalk me
In the hope I will be yours?
My journey can't last much longer
My strength begins to fail
Raven, surely you will be true
Until death overtakes me

19 Dance of the Firebird

Firebird (Igor Stravinsky)
Orchestral suite

The firebird is an imaginary being from Russian folk tales that is invariably described as a large bird with majestic red, yellow and orange plumage that glows brilliantly in the dark. It is associated with the phoenix, an enormous bird that the Greeks and Egyptians considered a demigod. According to legend, this being would burn in its own flames every 500 years, only to be born again from its ashes. For various cultures, the phoenix symbolizes immortality and resurrection, thus representing the hope that must never die in human beings.

The *Firebird* ballet, which is based on this clairvoyant and luminous being of Russian folklore, was met with public enthusiasm from the time it premiered.

One night, Prince Ivan gets lost in a dark enchanted forest. A firebird appears; Ivan is captivated by it and decides to chase it until he manages to catch it. The bird offers Ivan a magic feather that will save him in case of danger, in exchange for its freedom. Ivan accepts the deal and, in so doing, saves not only his own life but that of an entire kingdom ruled by Kashchei, an evil sorcerer.

All the descriptions of the firebird focus on its plumage rather than its song. By portraying it musically in his ballet, Stravinsky allows us to "see" the bursts of light that the bird emits in the darkness of the forest as well as imagine it being chased and captured.

20 Toy Symphony

Cassation for Orchestra and Toys (attributed to Leopold Mozart)

The cuckoo, the nightingale, the green woodpecker and the quail appear in this piece. They are represented by toy instruments, mainly whistles. Because they are easy to play, whistles have been very popular with children throughout time. Also, because of their sound resembling birdsong, many of these little instruments are shaped like a bird.

The bird call that mimics the cuckoo is a simple instrument. It has a mouthpiece and can produce two different sounds depending whether one of the two holes is covered or uncovered.

The bird call that mimics the nightingale and the quail is called a "water whistle." This instrument uses the movement of water, caused by blowing, to modify the pitch of the sound. The result is a modulated whistling similar to a bird's chirping. In addition to the whistles, you can also hear a trumpet, a drum, a triangle, a rattle and small bells.

Listening Guide

1 The Goldfinch

Il Gardellino (Antonio Vivaldi) ꞏ Concerto for flute and orchestra. Op 10/3, RV 428 Allegro.
Excerpt from the first movement. ꞏ Orchestra: Camerata Romana. ꞏ Conductor: Eugen Duvier

This piece is the first movement of the flute concerto entitled *Il Gardellino*. In the introduction, which showcases the string instruments, you will recognize the voice of the goldfinch, ever so softly at first, produced by the solo flute. Then, still represented by the flute, the goldfinch livens up and begins to sing, alternating indecisively between two notes and playing them faster and faster until they become a trill. Then, as if looking for the most appropriate sound to improvise, it chirps on the same two notes, leading to fast scales that finally set the tone. The first part ends as it began, with the strings repeating the opening melody. Throughout the movement, you will hear the continuous dialogue between the flute (the goldfinch) and the orchestra, which will at times sound like other birds answering.

2 Spring

La Primavera (Antonio Vivaldi) ꞏ Concerto for violin and orchestra. Op. 8/1 RV 269.
Exerpt from the first movement. ꞏ Orchestra: Musici di San Marco. ꞏ Conductor: Alberto Lizzio.
ꞏ Violin: A. Permovansky

In this famous first movement, you will hear the orchestra playing the renowned theme of *Spring,* first with considerable force, and then more softly, like an echo. After the introduction, you will hear the birdsong mimicked by the solo violinist, accompanied by two other violins. At the end of the bird passage, you will recognize the *Spring* theme played again by the orchestra.

3 Birdsong

Le chant des oiseaux (Clément Janequin) ꞏ Polyphonic song for 4 voices. Excerpt.
ꞏ Ensemble: I Fagiolini & Concordia

The human voice is the instrument used to imitate birdsong. You will first hear the basses begin the melody, followed by the tenors. A little further along, the contraltos make their entrance, and lastly, you will hear the sopranos. If you listen closely, you will notice that they all begin with the same melody, but as soon as one group begins, the other is already singing a different one. Soon, rather than words, you will hear peculiar syllables that are meant to mimic the song of various birds.

4 Melancholy

Cantus Arcticus (Einojuhani Rautavaara) 🐦 Concerto for birds and orchestra. Op 61. Excerpt.
🐦 Orchestra: Royal Scotish National. 🐦 Conductor: Hannu Lintu. 🐦 Piano: Laura Mikkola

At the beginning of the second movement, entitled *Melancholy,* you will hear the soft voice of actual larks recorded on magnetic tape. According to the composer, the "ghost" bird effect was achieved by lowering the entire recording by two octaves. When the orchestra comes in, you will see how how the sound "represents the uncertainty of the Nordic twilight, desolate and unsettling, where reality meets fantasy."

5 The Bird

Peter and the Wolf (Sergueï Prokofiev) 🐦 Flute solo. Op. 67. 🐦 Orchestra: English String Ochestra.
🐦 Conductor: Sir Yenudi Menuhin

You will hear a cheerful melody that mimics bird trills. Listen closely to the sound quality: high-pitched, soft and light. These characteristics will help you recognize the timbre of the flute and distinguish the other instruments, regardless of which piece you are listening to.

6 Hens and Roosters

The Carnival of the Animals (Camille Saint-Saëns) 🐓 A great zoological fantasy.
🐓 Orchestra: Süddeutsche Philharmonic Orchestra. 🐓 Conductor: Hanspeter Gmür

The piano and violins mimic the cackling and pecking of hens by repeating a series of notes that end with a drop. Listen closely to the rooster's voice, which comes in a little later with a trill from the second piano, and which seems momentarily to calm the coop the coop. However, he does not have the success he expects and repeats his cockadoodle doo. Listen closely: at the third call, you will notice that the clarinet has replaced the piano, but in vain. It is the nervous cackling of the hens that will prevail.

7 Aviary

The Carnival of the Animals (Camille Saint-Saëns) Flute piece.
Orchestra: Süddeutsche Philharmonic Orchestra. Conductor: Hanspeter Gmür

The flute will be the first to capture your attention, with its melodic line exhibiting extraordinary virtuosity that mimics the song of an unidentified bird. If you listen closely, you will hear the background sound created by the strings that conjure wind and the flapping of wings: the violins and violas are playing the same note, while the cello and bass perform a pizzicato between two notes. A little further along, you will hear the pianos join this celebration of sound, colour and movement with trills and scales.

8 The Swan

The Carnival of the Animals (Camille Saint-Saëns) Elegy for cello. Orchestra: Süddeutsche Philharmonic Orchestra. Conductor: Hanspeter Gmür

You will hear the swaying melodies against the steady rhythm of the pianos, evoking the gentle movement of water. You will also recognize the expressive voice of the cello, which will help you imagine an elegant swan gliding over its own reflection in the water.

9 Dance of the Little Swans

Swan Lake (Pyotr Ilyich Tchaikovsky) Ballet suite. Op. 20. Orchestra: Radio Symphony Orchestra Moscow. Conductor: Klaus-Peter Hahn

Listen to how Tchaikovsky makes use of the best musical resources melodically describing the little swans. You can notice the trembling rhythm of the accompaniment based on two alternating notes (F-C-F-C-F-C…). This way of producing sounds is called staccato; in this piece, it contributes to illustrating the clumsy walk of the baby swan. You will notice that the husky sound of the bassoon adds a touch of humour to the piece. You also hear the melody in staccato, performed by the oboe, whose soft but tinny timbre reminds us of the honking of the little swans.

10 Song of the Lark

Album for the Young (Pyotr Ilyich Tchaikovsky) 🐦 For piano. Op.39. 🐦 Piano: Idil Biret

In this simple piece, the piano mimics the song of the lark, repeating the same melodic motif with different notes in the high register. If you pay close attention, you will hear a second motif consisting of two sounds, one fast note that almost rises above the second, longer note (this note is called "appoggiatura"). Quickly going from one note to the other, the motif conjures the light, short hops of the lark on a branch.

11 Lark Ascending

Lark Ascending (Ralph Vaughan Williams) 🐦 Romance for violin and orchestra. Excerpt 🐦 Orchestra: English String Orchestra. 🐦 Conductor: William Boughton

To properly listen to this piece, you may have to turn up the volume because the piece opens with an almost inaudible pianissimo by the orchestra. Against this peaceful background, the lark, represented by the solo violin, takes flight. Its soft melody, which flows uninterrupted, calmly rises like a dream. It evokes the lovely song of the lark while calling to mind the ascent of the bird above the peaceful English countryside.

12 Ballet of the Unhatched Chicks

Pictures at an Exhibition (Modest Mussorgsky) 🐤 Piano suite. 🐤 Piano: Shura Cherkassky

We hear a string of short and slightly dissonant sounds, which bounce back rhythmically from one end of the piano to the other, depicting the jumping and pecking of chicks trying to get out of eggs. In the middle of the piece, the piano trills can be thought to represent the chicks testing their voice and perhaps asking their mother for help. The piece ends gracefully, repeating the amusing leaps heard at the beginning.

13 Toccata with Cuckoo Scherzo

Toccata con lo scherzo del cucco (Bernardo Pasquini) ✏ For harpsichord. Excerpt.
🐦 Harpsichord: Lorenzo Ghielmi

Pay close attention to the peculiar sound of the harpsichord. You may find it strange, since this instrument has been largely replaced by the piano. You will easily recognize the song of the cuckoo, even though it is slightly drowned out by the notes of the higher-pitched melody. While listening, think about the performer, whose fingers in the right hand are performing exercises in nimbleness while the left hand insistently repeats the cuckoo motif. At one point, you will notice that the two hands are playing the same thing, until the cuckoo moves to the treble register, with the left hand taking over the finger exercises.

14 The Cuckoo and the Nightingale

The Cuckoo and the Nightingale (George Frideric Handel) ✏ Concerto for organ and orchestra. No 13 in F Major. Allegro. Excerpt from the first movement. 🐦 Orchestra: Händel Festival Chamber Orchestra 🐦 Conductor: John Tinge. ✏ Organ: Johann Aratore

You will hear a dialogue between the orchestra—which offers a very lively theme—and the organ, with its highly distinctive consonance, repeating the same theme. A little further on, you will easily recognize the song of the cuckoo in the organ solo. The nightingale is not heard right away, but if you listen closely, you will hear its sustained trill when the soloist comes in, as the two notes of the cuckoo continue to be heard in the various instrument's registers. Soon after, the movement ends, as cheerfully as it began.

15 The Robin

Small Sketches of Birds (Olivier Messiaen) 🐦 For piano. Excerpt. 🐦 Piano: Hakon Austbø

Do not attempt to find a melody in this piece like the ones you are used to; this was not the composer's intention. The sequence of sounds and silences presents the bird as it is, without any embellishment. Listen closely to the complex harmonic combinations that will give you the strange impression that you are perceiving various auditory colours.

16 Papageno and Papagena

The Magic Flute (Wolfgang Amadeus Mozart) Duet for baritone and soprano. Orchestra: Falloni Orchestra Budapest. Conductor: Michael Halász. Baritone: Georg Tichy. Soprano: Hellen Kwon

In this duet with Papageno and Papagena, after a simple and innocent introduction by the strings, we hear Papageno, with his baritone voice, singing the syllable "pa" (the first syllable of the two names) repeatedly, in a shy call to his beloved that slowly gains confidence when the soprano Papagena answers him. The closer the sweethearts get to each other, repeating the same syllable faster and faster, the more the music, which is reminiscent of the chirping of birds, conveys the emotion felt by Papageno and Papagena upon their meeting, at first contained, and then overflowing.

17 Third Movement of Concerto No. 17

Piano Concerto No. 17 (Wolfgang Amadeus Mozart) For piano and orchestra. No 17, KV 453, in G Major. Allegretto. Excerpt from the third movement. Orchestra: Camerata Labacensis. Conductor: Kurt Redel. Piano: Leonart Hokanson

The orchestra introduces the starling's famous melody, so fresh and cheerful that it almost seems like a folk song (you can hum or whistle it in order not to forget it). This theme is made up of two phrases; each one is presented and repeated in order to penetrate the memory of the listener. Immediately after, you will distinguish the piano coming in with a variation of the first phrase of the same melody, and then, after it is repeated, you will hear the second phrase, played once again by the piano and, with very little variation, echoed by the orchestra. After it is repeated, you will hear the main theme played again by the orchestra, the piano playing a light and fast accompaniment. If you continue to listen closely, you will hear the melody transforming as the movement progresses, shifting among the piano and the various instruments of the orchestra, even changing in nature, but returning almost fully to its original state in the end.

18 The Raven

Winter Journey (Franz Schubert) 🐦 Lied for voice and piano. Op. 89 D. 91.
🐦 Baritone: Rudolf Knoll. 🐦 Piano: Hugo Steurer

As you listen, pay close attention to the high-pitched, repetitive and enveloping piano melody, which is sustained, even as the singer's voice comes in, to evoke the bird's unpleasant flight around the traveller's head. Saying the word *Krähe* ("raven"), the singer mimics the bird's voice. At the end of the song, you will hear the word *Grabe* ("grave"), which rhymes with *Krähe,* but which also expresses the young man's death wish.

19 Dance of the Firebird

Firebird (Igor Stravinsky) 🦅 Orchestral suite. 1910 version.
🦅 Orchestra: London Symphony Orchestra. 🦅 Conductor: Gennadi Rozhdestvensky

Listen closely to this piece; you will notice that the flute, once again, rises above the orchestra to convey the light and fascinating flight of the firebird, while the ascending glissandi of the piano and the harp depict Ivan's movements as he tries to catch it.

20 Toy Symphony

Toy Symphony (attributed to Leopold Mozart) 🐤 Cassation for Orchestra and Toys. Allegro. Excerpt.
🐤 Orchestra: Toronto Chamber Orchestra. 🐤 Conductor: Kevin Mallon

In this first movement of *Toy Symphony,* you will hear a cheerful melody played by the orchestra to the rhythm of a typical march (one-two, one-two). Following this, this, you can determine the metallic strokes of a few toys that keep time and then you will recognize the song of the cuckoo, performed by the birdcall, followed by the orchestra answering it. Soon after, when the music intensifies, the other toys liven up and begin to play, making a big racket with the orchestra. Throughout the piece, notice the contrast between the mechanical sound of the toy instruments and the pure and more fluid sound of the usual instruments.

The Composers

Antonio Vivaldi (1678–1741)

Italian composer from the baroque period. It was his father, a widely recognized violin virtuoso in Venice, who taught Vivaldi music. At the age of 25, Vivaldi was ordained a priest, but he would never exercise his functions. Nicknamed *il prete rosso,* "the red priest" because of the colour of his hair, Vivaldi held the positions of choir director and music director at Venice's Pio Ospedale Della Pietà, an institution that received young female orphans and offered them a high-level musical education, where he worked most of his life, alongside his many other activities. Under his direction, the Pio Ospedale orchestra became famous across Europe.

Among his countless vocal and instrumental compositions are close to 500 solo and orchestral concertos, all highly varied and uplifting. *The Four Seasons* are the best known.

Clément Janequin (c. 1485–1558)

French composer and priest from the Renaissance. Even though he never held a prominent position as a court or cathedral musician, he was one of the most popular composers of his time, and his songs were well loved and widely performed. Thanks to music printing, which had just been invented, his work quickly spread across Europe. *La bataille,* which vividly depicts the sounds and atmosphere of a battlefield, and *Le chant des oiseaux* (presented here) remain great favourites of modern-day Renaissance ensembles.

Einojuhani Rautavaara (1928)

A Finnish composer. Einojuhani Rautavaara and Jan Sibelius are Finland's best-known composers. A professor at the Sibelius Academy, Rautavaara was very prolific, composing a highly diverse range of works. In his youth, he experimented with all sorts of avant-garde genres before retaining only a few elements from these to create his own style. His music is characterized by his desire to create soundscapes.

Sergueï Prokofiev (1891–1956)

Twentieth century Russian composer. A child prodigy, he received his first music lessons from his mother, an amateur pianist. He composed his first opera, *The Giant,* at age nine. At 13, he entered the Saint Petersburg Conservatory (he remains the youngest student in the history of the conservatory), where he began to take an interest in the most avant-garde trends of the time. His first works, which were dissonant and deliberately raucous, earned him a reputation as an ultramodern musician. Following the October 1917 revolution, and in search of peace, for composing more than for ideological reasons, Prokofiev left the USSR and settled in the West. In 1933, after 15 years of exile, nostalgia led him to return to his country permanently.

In Soviet Russia, all artistic creations had to respect the dogmas of socialist realism. As a result, some of Prokofiev's works were considered too modern and were prohibited. He, therefore, adopted a more classical style, and the melodic element of his compositions became more prominent. Some of his best-known works are from this time: the children's tale *Peter and the Wolf,* as well as the ballets *Romeo and Juliet* and *Cinderella*. Sergueï Prokofiev passed away on March 5, 1953, the same day as Joseph Stalin.

Camille Saint-Saëns (1835–1921)

An extremely talented musician, Saint-Saëns was a piano virtuoso, organist, conductor, music critic and composer, but also a multifaceted intellectual. In addition to being greatly involved in music, he was also interested in various other disciplines, including geology, archaeology, botany and entomology. A member of the Société astronomique de France, he often planned his concerts to coincide with astronomical events.

His extensive work, which includes more than 400 compositions from almost every genre, was very eclectic, extremely classical and masterful but, at times, a little contrived. For this reason, he was deemed to be too academic. Saint-Saëns was the first renowned composer to compose music for a motion picture.

Pyotr Ilyich Tchaikovsky (1840–1893)

One of the most celebrated composers of the romantic period. He defined his work as the "musical confession of the soul."

From a very young age, Tchaikovsky was emotional and sensitive, earning him the nickname "porcelain child." He had a particular talent for music and, when he learned to play the piano, he would concentrate so hard when playing the instrument that he would end up exhausted, nervous and unable to sleep.

Out of family obligation, Tchaikovsky studied law and became a lawyer. However, at the age of 22, he decided to devote himself entirely to music and enrolled in the Saint Petersburg Conservatory. To earn a living, he taught piano and music theory. In 1885, Tchaikovsky's fame grew to soaring heights in Russia and the rest of Europe, before crossing the Atlantic to reach the United States. In 1890, he was invited to inaugurate Carnegie Hall in New York and, in 1893, was voted a member of the Académie des Beaux-Arts de l'Institut de France and obtained an honorary doctorate from the University of Cambridge.

Among his vast body of work, ever expressive and seductive, the three most famous are the three ballets, *Swan Lake, Sleeping Beauty* and *The Nutcracker*.

Ralph Vaughan Williams (1872–1958)

British composer and conductor known for his deep interest in English folklore and Renaissance music. It can be said that he was the main English representative of musical nationalism during the first half of the 20th century.

Vaughan Williams composed an extensive body of work, which includes symphonies, piano concertos, orchestral and choral compositions, various song collections, operas and incidental music.

Williams passed away in London at the age of 85. He rests in Westminster Abbey, near the famous English composer Sir Henry Purcell.

Modest Mussorgsky (1839–1881)

One of the most unique and influential Russian Nationalist composers of the 19th century. Mussorgsky lived on his parents' farm until the age of 10. His childhood left a lasting impression on him, and the composer soaked up all the sensibility and humour of the people in his village. Later on, in his musical body of work, he reproduced elements of Russian popular culture that had made such an impression on him as a child. It was his mother who taught him to play the piano, and he continued with excellent private teachers. Despite his musical vocation, Mussorgsky entered the Cadet School of the Guards of Saint-Petersburg to pursue a military career. At 18, he met the Russian Nationalist composers with whom he would form the group known as The Five. In 1858, he abandoned his military career to devote himself entirely to music, but in 1863, he was forced to take an administrative job to support himself. Mussorgsky was a self-taught composer. His bold and unorthodox harmonies, inspired by the repertoire of Russian folk music, influenced other foreign composers. His songs and operas reflected the desire to emulate the rhythms and tones of the Russian language.

Bernardo Pasquini (1637–1710)

Italian composer born in Massa, in Tuscany. Bernardo Pasquini moved to Rome as a young boy to study music. In 1663, he was named an organist of the Santa Maria Maggiore Basilica, and shortly after, of the church of Santa Maria in Aracoeli. He later entered the service of prince Giambattista Borghese. He made his mark as a virtuoso harpsichordist and choir master. He frequently collaborated with Arcangelo Corelli and Alessandro Scarlatti to perform concerts in various cities across Italy. His body of work includes numerous vocal compositions, mainly oratorios, operas and cantatas. His harpsichord compositions are the most enjoyed of his works today.

George Frideric Handel (1685–1759)

German-born British composer. He is one of the most influential musicians of the baroque period and of all time. Handel was an extraordinarily prolific musician whose work influenced all musical styles of his time, even though he composed mainly operas and oratorios. Thanks to him, these two genres reached their golden age.

At a remarkably young age, Handel showed tremendous talent, but his father, a court barber surgeon, did not consider music a respectable profession and decided that his son would be a lawyer. It is said that a young George would sneak off to the attic at night to practice on a discarded harpsichord. It is also said that it was the Prince of Saxe, informed of the child's genius, who convinced the father to allow Handel to take official lessons.

At age 17, Handel was already an organist at a church in his native town, but this position was not a good match for his tastes or ambition. Following study tours in Germany and Italy, he settled down in London in 1712; he would remain there for the rest of his life. *The Messiah,* composed in 1741 in only 24 days, is one of the most famous oratorios in the history of music.

Handel rests in the venerable Westminster Abbey.

Olivier Messiaen (1908–1992)

French composer, organist and ornithologist. Demonstrating his talent early on, he began composing at the age of seven, at the same time as he started taking piano lessons. He entered the Conservatoire de Paris at age 11, where he studied organ and composition. He was intensely religious and held the position of organist at the Sainte-Trinité de Paris church from 1931 until his death. He was a prisoner during World War II, and when he realized that other musicians were also detained, he composed *Quatuor pour la fin du Temps* (quartet for the end of time) for the piano, violin, cello, and clarinet, the instruments played by his cellmates. The premier was performed by Messiaen and his fellow detainees before an audience of prisoners and guards. Following his release, he was named professor of harmony, and, in 1966, of composition, at the Conservatoire de Paris. Among his best-known students were Pierre Boulez, Karlheinz Stockhausen and Iannis Xenakis.

Messiaen was fascinated by birdsong and said that birds were the best musicians. He even considered himself an ornithologist, on the same level as he did a composer. He would spend long hours in nature listening to birds and transcribing their songs in special journals, in which he would record details such as the type of bird, the time, the location and the environment. He managed to distinguish the song of over 400 species.

Wolfgang Amadeus Mozart (1756–1791)

Austrian composer. He is the defining musician of the classical period, if not of all time.

At the age of three, Wolfgang Amadeus's favourite pastime was searching for, in his own words, "notes that love each other" on his father's clavichord. He began composing at the age of four, even before he could write. Wolfgang possessed exceptional talent, a will to learn and unmatched enthusiasm. His father, Leopold, himself an excellent musician, quickly realized that his son was a musical genius, and he abandoned his career as a violinist to devote himself entirely to Wolfgang's musical education. At the age of six, Wolfgang began making long trips in uncomfortable stagecoaches to perform concerts. His musical talent was acclaimed in the most powerful courts of Europe. It is estimated that, over the course of his life, Mozart spent 3,720 days travelling, which amounts to a total of 10 years! This is how Mozart spent his youth, establishing himself and gaining a solid musical culture and training that enriched his natural talent. However, the hoped-for wealth was not to be.

At the age of 26, Wolfgang settled in Vienna, the capital of Austria, to try his hand as an independent musician, something that was completely novel at the time. He would spend his adult life struggling to earn a living, teaching piano and producing commissioned compositions. Worn out by continuous musical production, disappointed by the lack of public response to his music and almost destitute, Mozart passed away on December 5, 1791, just before his 36th birthday.

He composed close to 600 works of extraordinary quality, in all the styles of his time.

Franz Schubert (1797–1828)

Born in Vienna, Franz Schubert was the 12th of 14 children of a modest schoolmaster. At the age of five, he began taking piano, violin and singing lessons; his teachers were stunned by the ease with which he learned to play at such a young age. Schubert, who passed away at the tender age of 31, was one of the first composers of the romantic period. His talent grew in the shadow of Beethoven, whom he profoundly admired. He was overshadowed during his life, and it was only after his death that his art began to be recognized and to gain the admiration of critics and the public. Schubert passed away one year after Beethoven and, as per his final wishes, was buried next to him.

Schubert devoted much of his creative energy to lyrical song (lied), an immensely popular genre in the romantic period. A prominent German singer summarized the career of the Austrian composer as follows: "When song and poetry arrived on the earth, they were personified in Franz Schubert."

Igor Stravinsky (1882–1971)

Russian composer who became a naturalized French citizen in 1936 and naturalized American citizen in 1945. A musical figurehead of the 20th century, he passed away just before his 89th birthday. This longevity allowed him to experience and create a wide range of musical trends and to distinguish himself in every style.

After obtaining his law degree in 1905, Igor Stravinsky studied composition for five years with Nicolaï Rimski-Korsakov, then director of the Saint Petersburg Conservatory. Stravinsky's first compositions sparked the interest of Sergei Diaghilev, director of the Ballets Russes (a ballet company that aimed to showcase the cultural richness of Russia to all of Europe), who commissioned the score for *Firebird*. In the years that followed, he continued his collaboration with Diaghilev, first composing the ballet *Petrushka* (1911) and then *The Rite of Spring* (1913), whose originality and primitive force caused a scandal at the premier. The intense dissonance and strong asymmetrical rhythms created such an uproar in the audience that the dancers could not even hear the orchestra. Shortly thereafter, however, the work enjoyed international acclaim. Despite the success of these three ballets, Stravinsky abandoned the Russian Nationalist style to take on new challenges. Upon his passing, which occurred almost 60 years later in the United States, Stravinsky left behind a large number of works of all genres: ballets, operas, symphonies, concertos and sonatas, in all musical styles. As per his last wishes, he was buried in Venice, near his old friend Sergei Diaghilev.

Johann Georg Leopold Mozart (1719–1787)

German musician, father of the famous composer Wolfgang Amadeus Mozart, himself a talented violinist. Not very well liked during his life, he was criticized after his death for having been an overprotective and tyrannical father to his prodigal son.

He was recognized for his compositions and as a music teacher, particularly of violin. His work *A Treatise on the Fundamental Principles of Violin Playing,* published in Augsburg in 1765, has been translated into several languages.

Glossary of Musical Terms

4 voices: Refers to four groups of people each singing a separate melody. Human voices can be classified into six groups, three for women and three for men. Women's voices include soprano (the highest voice), mezzo-soprano (the middle voice) and contralto (the lowest voice). For men, the voices include tenor (the highest voice), baritone (the middle voice) and bass (the lowest).

Ballet: Musical composition intended to be performed by dancers.

Bassoon: A woodwind instrument in the double-reed family, considered the bass of the oboe family.

Cassation: Originates from the German word *Gasse,* "street," where this type of music was generally played. Work for orchestra with no defined form, made up of various movements, the first of which is often a march.

Cello: Bowed string instrument from the violin family whose size and register are between that of the viola and the bass. To play it, the cellist holds the instrument between his or her legs and rubs the strings with a bow.

The cello is traditionally considered the string instrument that most resembles the human voice. Throughout the history of music, numerous works have been composed for this instrument due to the warmth of its tone, its versatility and its expressivity.

Clarinet: Black woodwind instrument. Its timbre is rich in nuance and expressive possibilities. It is the most nimble instrument of the orchestra, after the flute, as well as one of the most versatile.

Concerto: Composition in which a solo instrument has a dialogue with a group of instruments (the orchestra). The solo instrument (the soloist) plays the melody while the orchestra plays the accompaniment. These compositions, which appeared in the baroque period, are divided into three parts (movements). Generally, the first movement is quite fast, the second, a little slow, and the last movement is even faster than the first.

Counterpoint: Comes from the Latin term, *punctus contra punctum,* meaning "note against note." Composition technique based on the superimposition of two or more melodic lines. Counterpoint is considered the technical foundation of polyphony.

Dissonance: Combination of two or more notes that sounds harsh or unpleasant.

Duet: Musical composition for two vocalists. In the case of two instrumentalists, it is generally called a duo. During the second half of the 18th century, and particularly in the 19th century, the aria (for a solo vocalist) was slowly replaced by the duet as the main composition of the opera. The duet was preferred because of its dynamism, a result of the opposition and contrast between two characters.

Elegy: Poetic and evocative free-form composition.

Fantasy: Free-form musical composition that is set apart by its imaginative and improvisational character. It offers the composer extraordinary musical expression by eliminating the restrictions inherent in other, more rigid traditional forms.

Glissando: An Italian term from the French word *glisser,* "to slide." It denotes a rapid execution of a scale toward the highest note (ascending) or the lowest (descending). In keyboard instruments such as the piano, the back of the hand is made to slide across the white keys.

Harmony: Simultaneous organization of various sounds.

Harp: String instrument consisting of a sound box with a series of strings of different lengths strung between the lower and upper part of the frame. The strings can be plucked using one's fingers or a plectrum.

Harpsichord: Keyboard instrument widely used in the baroque period. Contrary to the piano, the harpsichord has a string mechanism that is plucked using a plectrum, which produces a soft, slightly metallic sound more resembling that of a harp or guitar. Many pieces written for this instrument are now performed on the piano.

Interval: Distance between two sounds.

Legato: Stems from the Italian word *legato,* "linked." A way of producing sounds without detaching the notes.

Lied: Comes from the German word *lied,* "song," lieder in the plural. A short vocal composition accompanied on the piano, of folk origin with a poetic touch. Well suited to the expression of emotions, this genre flourished during the Romantic period. The lied is characterized by brevity, relinquishing virtuosity and close relationship to poetry. The melody and accompaniment aim to translate the words of the poem into musical elements.

March: Musical piece intended to mark the steps of a small or large group. The best-known are military marches, but there are also funeral and wedding marches.

Measure: Rhythmic division of a musical piece into equal parts.

Microtone: smaller than a semitone, which is the smallest interval in Western music.

Motif: Short melodic or rhythmic idea that is the primary unit of a musical fragment.

Oboe: Woodwind instrument with a conical bore whose sound is produced through the vibration of a double-reed when air is blown into it. Its timbre is characterized by a sound that is penetrating, harsh, slightly tinny, soft and very expressive.

Octave: Distance between two sounds separated by seven consecutive degrees (for example, C-D-E-F-G-A-B-C). The frequency of the lower sound is half that of the higher sound.

Opera: Classical music genre that began in Italy at the end of the Renaissance and at the beginning of the Baroque period (1600). It is defined as a "theatrical piece put to music." The dialogues are sung and accompanied by an orchestra.

Oratorio: Dramatic lyrical composition dealing with sacred topics, with choir and orchestra.

Organ: Keyboard instrument with no strings, contrary to the harpsichord and the piano. Sounds are produced by wind moving through pipes of different lengths (from a few millimetres to several metres). This is why the organ is considered a wind instrument. Organs are generally very large instruments, some of them even covering an entire wall of a church. They have two to six keyboards, each of which gives a different colour to the same notes, and pedals. Mastering the various aspects of the organ mechanism requires full coordination of the eyes, ears, hands and feet, a complex process.

The organ was one of the most popular instruments of medieval times, the Renaissance and the Baroque period.

Pianissimo: Italian term used in music to indicate the lowest sound intensity; very softly.

Piano: Keyboard string instrument invented around 1700. Pressing a key causes a hammer to strike the corresponding string and produce a sound. The word piano is an abbreviation of pianoforte (from the Italian *piano,* "quiet," and *forte,* "loud"), which refers to the piano's ability to produce sounds of different intensities depending on the force applied to the keys, something which was not possible with its predecessors (the harpsichord and the clavichord), which could only produce one volume. The piano is the most significant instrument of Western music. In addition to the immense quantity of works composed for the piano and all its expressive possibilities—it is the instrument that can produce the most sounds at

the same time—, the piano is an essential element in the study of basic musical knowledge. It is an irreplaceable tool in the composition process.

Pizzicato: Originates from the Italian word *pellizcado,* "pinched." A sound obtained by pinching the strings of a bow instrument with one's fingers.

Polyphonic song: Polyphony, which means "many sounds" in Greek, is a form of composition that combines various independent melodies that differ from one another at all times. The challenge with polyphonic composition lies in harmonizing various melodies. It is interesting to note that if you tried to follow four conversations at the same time it would make your head spin but with music, when you hear four different melodies you immediately get a sense of wholeness.

Register: Range of a voice or instrument (from the highest pitch to the lowest).

Romance: Simple and moving instrumental composition.

Rondo: A term meaning round, or circle dance. A musical form based on the repetition of a theme. In a rondo, the principal theme (A) is repeated at least three times. It is alternated with various musical themes or couplets. The structure of the rondo is, therefore,
A B A C A.

Scale: Series of sounds produced in ascending or descending order. The most widely known scale is "do-re-mi-fa-so-la-ti-do."

Scherzo: This term originates from the Italian word *scherzo,* "game," or "joke." Beginning in the Classical period, it is a name given to a musical piece, or a movement from a larger piece, for example, a symphony. However, in the *Toccata con lo scherzo del cucco* (composed before the classical period), *scherzo* refers to the cuckoo's game.

Score: Transcription of the notes of a musical work.

Staccato (from the Latin *staccare,* "detach"): Form of musical articulation that consists in cutting the note shorter than its original value.

Suite: Instrumental composition made up of a series of short sections or movements. The suite, which appeared in the 16th century, includes a series of folk songs and dances generally in the same key. While they are all separate pieces, these songs and dances nevertheless combine to present strong contrasts between slow and fast tempos as well as majestic and cheerful modes. Today, the suite is simply a work made up of a series of short pieces with a common element.

Symphony: Orchestral piece, generally divided into four movements each with a different speed and structure. It is one of the most prominent forms in classical music.

Theme and variations: Musical form in which a fundamental melody is repeated throughout the piece but in altered form. There are several ways to alter a melody: by adding ornamental notes or by varying the rhythm, accompaniment or even the instrument that produces it. In doing so, the melody becomes so different that you have to listen closely to recognize it.

Theme: This is the main idea, generally a recognizable melody, upon which all or part of a composition is based.

Timbre: Sound quality that allows us to distinguish two instruments or two voices from one another, even if they are producing the same note.

Toccata: Stems from the Italian word *toccare,* "to touch." A Baroque musical piece composed for keyboard instruments, generally showcasing musical ability.

Tone: The longest distance between two conjunct degrees of the scale. Between C and D, there is one tone; however, between E and F, there is a semitone.

Transcription: Conversion of spoken language into written form. In this publication, it is the conversion of sounds heard in nature into written music.

Violin: Smallest of the string family, and one of the most popular instruments. The beauty of its tone and its impressive richness of expression make it an ideal solo instrument, treasured by musicians and music lovers for centuries. It also plays an important role in an orchestra. Together with the larger and deeper sounding members of its family, the violin is the heart of the orchestra. This instrument is played by rubbing a bow against its strings. It can also be played by plucking its strings with one's fingers to produce a sound called *pizzicato*.

The violin, a descendant of the larger and deeper sounding viola family (viola díamore, viola da gamba), dates back to 1550 A.D. On the surface, the violin is one of the most accessible modern instruments: it is made up of a varnished wood sound box, a long neck and four very taut strings. Appearances can be deceiving, however… the violin is made up of around 70 pieces.

Virtuosity: Technical ability of the instrumentalist.

Timeline of composers and periods

	1450	1500	1550	16
Janequin (1485–1558)				
Pasquini (1637–1710)				
Vivaldi (1678–1741)				
Handel (1685–1759)				
Leopold Mozart (1719–1787)				
Wolfgang Amadeus Mozart (1756–1791)				
Schubert (1797–1828)				
Saint-Saëns (1835–1921)				
Mussorgsky (1839–1881)				
Tchaikovsky (1840–1893)				
Vaughan Williams (1872–1958)				
Stravinsky (1882–1971)				
Prokofiev (1891–1956)				
Messiaen (1908–1992)				
Rautavaara (1928–)				

Renaissance

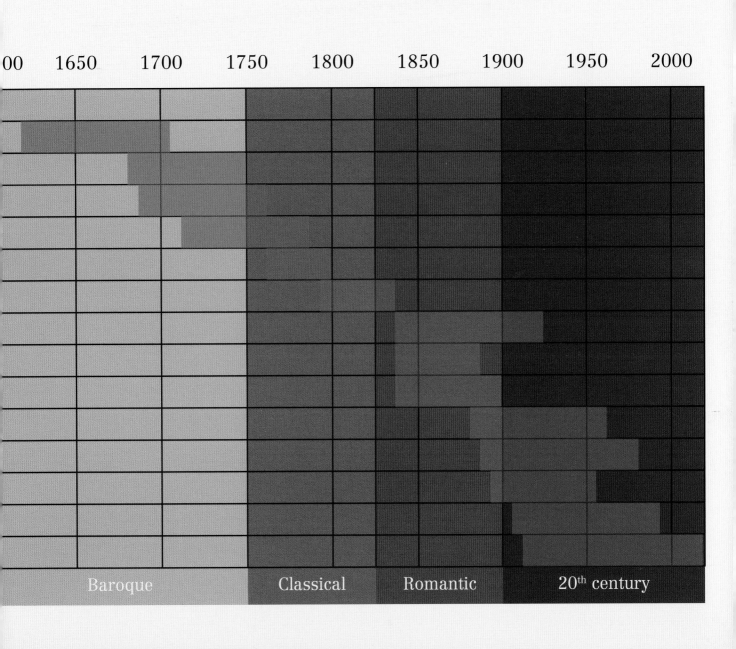

Music selection and explanatory notes Ana Gerhard

Illustrations Cecilia Varela

Translation from Spanish to English Helène Roulston and Sabrina Diotalevi
for Service d'édition Guy Connolly

Graphic design Francisco Ibarra Meza and Stéphan Lorti

Copy editing Ruth Joseph

First published in Spanish as *Las aves - Introducción a la música de concierto*
© 2010 Ana Gerhard (text), © 2010 Cecilia Varela (illustrations),
© 2010 Editorial Océano S.L., Barcelona (spain)

Master recordings under license from Grupo Eurogy de México

www.thesecretmountain.com

2013 The Secret Mountain (Folle Avoine Productions)
ISBN-10 2-923163-89-3 / ISBN-13 978-2-923163-89-5